The
Costume
Party

The
Costume
Party

W. B. Park

LITTLE, BROWN AND COMPANY

BOSTON   TORONTO

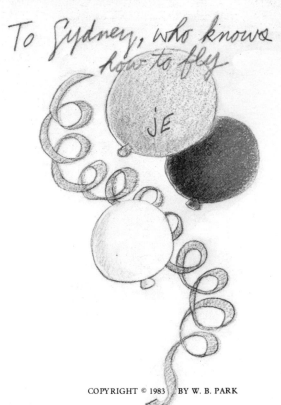

To Sydney, who knows how to fly

JE

FIRST EDITION

Library of Congress Cataloging in Publication Data

Summary: When the guests at her costume party
unmask, Shirley discovers that the mystery guest,
dressed as a bear, really is a bear.

[1. Parties — Fiction. 2. Bears — Fiction]
I. Title.

PZ7.P22145Co 1982   [E]   82-4693
ISBN 0-316-69077-5 (lib. bdg.)

WOR

*Published simultaneously in Canada
by Little, Brown and Company (Canada) Limited*

PRINTED IN THE UNITED STATES OF AMERICA

It was the night of the party.
Shirley could hardly w̲...
all her friends in t̲...

There were roller skaters

and a chef

and a pretty ballet dancer.

Shirley was happy.
Everyone she invited had come.
"Let's play some games!"
she cried.
Just then the doorbell rang.

Shirley opened the door.
There stood a huge bear!
"Ohhh!" said all the guests.
But Shirley saw something.
The bear had a big zipper
down his front.
"Don't worry," she said.
"It's only a costume."

Who could be inside?
No one could guess.
Shirley took the bear's paw.
"Come in," she said.
"What a good costume!"
The bear just smiled.

10

First they played hide-and-seek.
The bear was "It."
In no time he found everyone.
"He must have peeked,"
said the sheep.

"Simon Says" was the next game.
"Touch the sky!" said Shirley.
"You didn't say 'Simon Says,'"
said the bear.
"Didn't his arms go up a little?"
asked a roller skater.

14

Leapfrog was fun.
Then the bear took his turn.

"I don't want to play anymore,"
said the dog.

They tried a new game.
But the bear pinned the tail
on the wrong donkey.

Next came the game
the pig liked best.
It was the pie-eating contest.

The bear ate ten pies.
The pig ate five pies.
The bear wanted more.
The pig was mad.
"I should have won," he said.

"Let's bob for apples,"
said the ballet dancer.
She was very good at bobbing.
The bear went first.
He didn't seem to know the rules.

Shirley had to do something.
The bear was spoiling her party.
"Time to take off our masks!"
she cried.

Everyone unmasked quickly.
Who was inside the bear costume?
They all watched
as he took hold of his zipper...

...and pulled it right off!
"Oh, no!" the guests cried.
"It really *is* a bear!"
They all ran away.

26

Shirley didn't run away.
She was too angry.
"You ruined my party,"
she said to the bear.
"I'm sorry," said the bear.
"I've never been to a party before."
I'm new here. I was lonesome."

The bear looked very unhappy.
Shirley started to feel bad.
"Well," she said.
"I guess you can stay.
But you have to be good."
"I'll try," said the bear.

All the guests came back.
The bear was good.
He said "Please" and "Thank you."
He almost always remembered
to wait his turn.

Everyone began to like the bear.
They gave him first prize
for the best costume!
When the party was over
everyone was glad the bear had come.

Everyone except the pig.
He was busy practicing
for next year's pie-eating contest.